For all those who swear it's true
(with special thanks to believers
Rebecca, Alex, Lizzy, and Chloë)

SIMON & SCHUSTER BOOKS FOR YOUNG READERS • An imprint of Simon & Schuster Children's Publishing Division • 1230 Avenue of the Americas, New York, New York 10020 • Copyright © 2013 by Scott Magoon • All rights reserved, including the right of reproduction in whole or in part in any form. • SIMON & SCHUSTER BOOKS FOR YOUNG READERS is a trademark of Simon & Schuster, Inc. • For information about special discounts for bulk purchases, please contact Simon & Schuster Special Sales at 1-866-506-1949 or business@simonandschuster.com. • The Simon & Schuster Speakers Bureau can bring authors to your live event. For more information or to book an event, contact the Simon & Schuster Speakers Bureau at 1-866-248-3049 or visit our website at www.simonspeakers.com. • Book design by Chloë Foglia • The text for this book is set in ITC Usherwood Std. • The illustrations for this book are rendered digitally. • Manufactured in China • 1112 SCP

10 9 8 7 6 5 4 3 2 1

Library of Congress Cataloging-in-Publication Data • Magoon, Scott. • The boy who cried Bigfoot! / Scott Magoon. — 1st ed. • p. cm. • "A Paula Wiseman Book." • Summary: Ben has so often tried to convince people he has seen Bigfoot that when a real yeti arrives and borrows his bicycle, no one comes to see if Ben is telling the truth.

ISBN 978-1-4424-1257-6 (hardcover) • [1. Honesty—Fiction. 2. Yeti—Fiction.] I. Boy who cried wolf. II. Title. • PZ7.M31266513Boy 2012 • [E]—dc22 • 2010031149 • ISBN 978-1-4424-6866-5 (eBook)

THE BOY WHO CRIED BIGFOOT!

By Scott Magoon

A Paula Wiseman Book
Simon & Schuster Books for Young Readers
NEW YORK   LONDON   TORONTO   SYDNEY   NEW DELHI

This is the story of my friend Ben and how we first met.

This is Ben.

Ben liked to tell stories.

He liked to tell stories . . .

All that practice made him a pretty
good storyteller.

He even used props. What a tenacious little fellow he was.

People came from all over town to see Bigfoot.
They waited and they waited, but the creature
never appeared.

"He walked right
through here, see?"

After many hours with no sightings, everyone suspected that Ben had made it all up.

"Bigfoot isn't real."

"He IS real!
His feet were THIS BIG!
He was right here.
I saw him!"

"I don't ever remember crossing
paths with *you*, Littlefoot," I said.

I didn't normally talk to a Littlefoot. But there was something about this Ben I liked. He was a determined fellow. I also liked his bike! I asked, "Mind if I take it for a ride?"

"Buh-buh-Bigfoot?"

sniff sniff

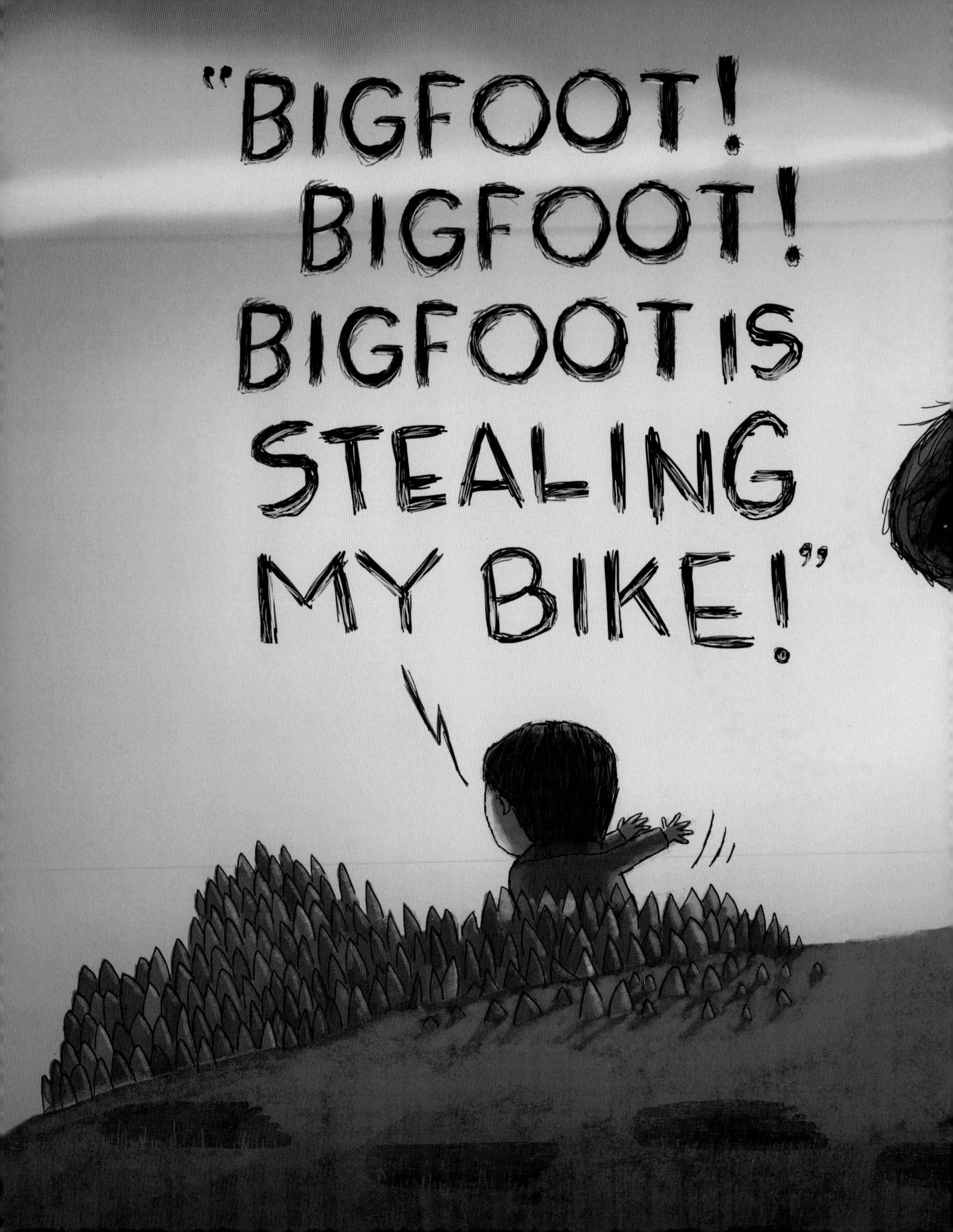
"BIGFOOT! BIGFOOT! BIGFOOT IS STEALING MY BIKE!"

"Coming with?"

Alas, no one believed Ben anymore.
No one came running.
It seemed Ben found being alone to
be a little scary.

Fortunately for Ben, he wasn't alone for long.

"Ben, where are you?
Come home, it's time for dinner!"

And it was time for
me to go home too.

"I'm sorry I created such a ruckus," Ben said. "But I really *did* see him, Mom."
"Oh, Ben," she said. "Let's go home."

So Ben and his family went home and had a hot meal.
I don't know what a hot meal is, but I do know that Ben
learned the importance of always telling the truth.
And he wanted everyone to know he really *had* seen me.

So the next morning, he set out to
prove it.
What a tenacious fellow he is.